Fraser!

Not Way Too TALL After All!

Written by Joy M. O'Hora©

Illustrated by Mairead Brennan

To Claire,
who loved children.

About 1,000 sleeps ago, Fraser, a tall fir tree, stood in a small pretty forest, on the edge of a busy town.

Every December, as soon as school finished for the Holidays, townspeople visited. They wanted to choose a fir tree as their Christmas or Holiday tree.

Peoples of all ages, families of all shapes and sizes, big and small, travelled to the forest!

Some families had brothers and sisters, some had a Mom or Dad, some had both. Some kids arrived with their Gran or Grandad and some had two Dads and two Moms.

On days the
families arrived,
the pretty forest
was filled with
laughter, colour
and excitement!
Fraser's branches
shook in
anticipation,
he waited to be
chosen.

Fraser waited...
patiently.

Fraser knew about the Holidays and Christmas from nature walks the junior school children took with their teachers.

As the long line of kids wound their way around the forest, their teachers explained how some of the trees would, someday, be Christmas trees and that it could take 10 years or more for the littlest trees to grow.

The teachers described how the trees would be all lit up with twinkly lights, and best of all, crowned with a big star on the very tippy-top branch.

Oh, how Fraser longed to be picked.

Holiday Season after Holiday Season, kids would run excitedly up to him, shouting back at the adults, "THIS ONE! *Pick this one! Its branches go WAY way way up high!*" but the adults always chuckled, shook their heads kindly and declared Fraser to be "*Way Too Tall!*"

Sometimes, the littlest kids hugged Fraser and... well... that made Fraser feel better.

The seasons passed. Big winds whooshed, snows swirled, all around the forest, then settled softly. Rain pelted down, softening the earth, the sun warmed and brightened everything in the forest.

Fraser stood on... he waited, patiently, still, deeply rooted to his mother earth... friends with all the birds and flowers of the forest.

As the seasons changed, Fraser kept growing, his branches stretching right-up to the clouds or clear blue sky by day and the navy black star-filled sky by night. Fraser dreamed about reaching those stars and wearing a star on his top branch.

Fraser was now the tallest tree in the forest for miles and miles! Fraser felt so alive, so fresh, breathing out his pure pine-scented air for every living creature, plant and townspeople to enjoy.

More Holiday Seasons came and went and went again.

Fraser stood on patiently, waiting, watching all the other trees in the forest getting picked.

Do you know...
Sometimes, when we are patient and grateful, just standing still, change happens all by itself... without any fuss or bother.

And... one wintry afternoon Fraser got a huge surprise. Just as dusk was settling for yet another day, a group of people dressed in bright yellow overalls, arrived in a **ginormous, long red truck**. They wore black heavy boots. They looked serious.

They immediately spotted Fraser - the tallest tree in the forest. They surrounded him...

Fraser had been chosen!!

Fraser's branches swelled with pride, he took a big deep breath as the yellow-overall people took out their saws and cut him away from his mother earth.
It did not hurt.

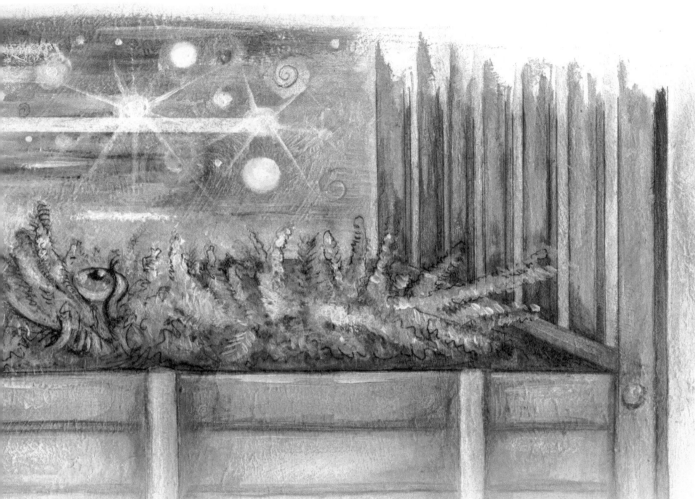

After much huffing, puffing, hefting and hollering, Fraser found himself laying down in the back of that **long ginormous truck**. The navy black night sky streaked with yellow lights, raced by.

After a snooze Fraser was
hoisted to a standing position
again, his roots no longer
planted in mother earth but
plunged into a bucket of
ice-cold water. It was
refreshing.

Fraser wondered where
he was. This home was
nothing like the homes
described by the
teachers on
nature walks...

Fraser wondered when the one big star he longed
for, would appear for him to wear...

Fraser's new home, was, in fact, the large entrance hall of a block of offices downtown.

The building had very high ceilings...

It was perfect, just perfect for him.

All day long
people dressed in
suits dashed by
Fraser, speaking
on, or gazing at
phones, dazed,
and distracted,
everyone lost in
their own world.

At night, the building was empty of dashing-by people, except for Don, the Security Guard, who sat in a little cubicle near Fraser. Don read his newspaper or scrolled, bored, looking at his phone! Occasionally, Don had a little sleep, with his head resting on his newspaper, the pages fluttered softly up and down as he snored gently at his desk.

Again, Fraser stood patiently, waiting. Fraser felt pleased... a couple of sleeps later his patience and gratitude were rewarded...

Bright and early, two ladies - one short, one tall, who normally dashed by, arrived carrying a big sign. They placed the sign right next to Fraser...

The sign read:

"Help our Junior School, Buy a Little Star, Decorate our Tree!"

And do you know... the other dashing-by people did
just that... after all, it was the Holidays!

Soon, Fraser, whose top branch almost touched the
ceiling of the tall building (but not quite) was all
dressed. Each branch covered with small bright,
helpful stars shining, twinkling, winking.

Fraser beamed, he was a golden shimmering light
of powerful patience. Fraser was majestic!

And something else happened...
All, absolutely ALL of the dashing-by people stopped,
they stood, still. They put down their phones and
stood, just like Fraser in the forest. They stared up at
him in awe and gratitude.

The dashing-by people used their phones to take photos of themselves and their friends with Fraser, oh how they all laughed! It was the jolliest of times.

Best of all, the school kids came to visit. They sang songs, and the dashing-by people joined in. The kids were rewarded with hot chocolate and red and white candy canes.

Then, the smallest child with the help of Don, climbed the big sturdy ladder and placed the star, that Fraser had so wanted, on his tippy-top branch.

Everyone clapped and cheered, then sighed and declared Fraser to be the best tree ever!

Fraser smiled to himself. The children and the dashing-by people could not *see* his smile, they could *feel* his smile and they smiled too and at each other.

Fraser was **Not Way Too TALL After All!**

The days passed, the dashing-by people left to go home for the holidays. Fraser was becoming sleepier with each passing day. When Don finally locked up the building for the holidays, as he tipped his cap at Fraser to say goodbye, Fraser was finding it hard to breathe.

Uprooted from his forest earth, with just the warm air of the building, Fraser's energy was slowly, but surely slipping away.

After a few more sleeps, Fraser's top branch, that one that almost touched the ceiling, but not quite, dipped over. The big, beautiful star that held on his tippy top branch, tumbled to the cold shiny floor below, it bounced and rolled just a little, then came to a stop, unbroken.

Fraser then went to sleep forever.

His job was done...

When the Holiday Season ended, those same people in bright yellow overalls came and laid Fraser in that same ginormous truck. They brought Fraser back to his forest!

There, along with all the other now fast asleep forever Holiday trees, Fraser was recycled, and all his goodness, patience and majesty were sprinkled far and wide, right back on his mother earth, to nourish and grow more trees.

So... no matter what kind of tall or small you are, every tall or small is here for a special reason. There is a place for everyone, all sizes, in this world of ours.

Reach for your star... the world is perfect for you, and you are perfect for this world!

The End... *until a new fir tree grows,*
maybe as tall as Fraser... or smaller... maybe.

Lightning Source UK Ltd.
Milton Keynes UK
UKHW050326120921
390400UK00004B/6

An early shot of J-type production at Adderley Park, Birmingham around 1950. A far cry from today's robotised assembly lines!

Published by

PAST
Masters

GW00458474

The J-type Van

A Classic Light Commercial

by
Harvey Pitcher

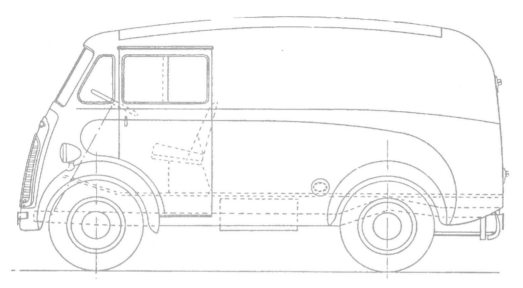

©2002 Harvey Pitcher

Published by
Past Masters
31 Queenswood Road
Moseley
Birmingham (Home of the J-type)
B13 9AU
United Kingdom

Length* :	11 ft 7⅝ in (3546mm)
Width :	5 ft 3¾ in (1620mm)
Height ** :	6 ft 7 in (2007mm)
Wheelbase :	7 ft 2 in (2184mm)
Load Bed height :	1 ft 11½ in (597mm)

*Without bumpers (which were listed as standard on Export models, but fitted at extra cost for Home market)

**Dependant upon wheel size used, and other variables such as whether a roof-top vent is fitted. Coachbuilt bodywork can be considerably higher.

ISBN 0-9543982-0-3

A Brief History!

The J-type was introduced at the 1948 Commercial Motor Show at Earls Court. The pre-production van which Morris-Commercial exhibited on their stand at the show differed in many details from the production vehicle that was to follow in the autumn of 1949.

The 'easiclean' wheels gave way to pressed steel disc items, whilst the front grille, headlamp/sidelight units, and many other items were redesigned before full production commenced. The 1949 Geneva Commercial Vehicle Show van still sported 'easiclean' wheels, but also had a chromed front bumper with a shape unlike anything seen subsequently.

Morris-Commercial had introduced the fully forward control 15/20 cwt 'PV' model in 1939, although few were manufactured before the outbreak of the Second World War brought production to a halt. Production resumed in 1945.

Prior to the introduction of the J-type, light vans had been the preserve of Morris Motors at Cowley, another part of the same Nuffield empire, which had been manufacturing vans based on their car chassis

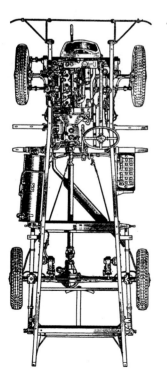

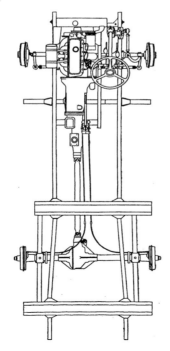

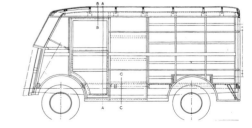

A side view of the 15/20cwt PV

Chassis layouts for the 'Series II' (far left) and the J-type, which closely followed the earlier model's configuration even down to the positioning of the battery and the petrol tank (not shown in this illustration) - more commonly on the right side of the vehicle on previous Morris-Commercials.

since 1924. By the mid-'30s Morris was manufacturing a 10 cwt van, the 'Series II', which, although not fully forward control, had many similarities with the J-type that was to follow, mirroring its overall compact size and its offset engine/differential. The 'Series II' was succeeded by the 'Series Y', which kept the offset chassis layout. This layout was not unique to the Morris Organisation, as the natural competitor to the company's 10 cwt offerings - the Ford E83W van - was similarly 'lop-sided' mechanically.

Another vehicle that must have influenced the designers working on the J-type was the Trojan 12 cwt Senior. This was fully forward control - even if the powers that be at Trojan felt it necessary to add an empty, vestigial bonnet to the van's front end. This 'bonnet' was empty because the van had a centrally mounted horizontal four-cylinder two-stroke engine attached to a gearbox with only two forward speeds! With a power output of 15¾ bhp it was hardly going to set the tarmac alight!

Above:
Morris-Commercial's post-war front end house style.

Left: A 1936 Trojan Senior, very similar in size and proportion to a J-type!

Left: A prewar Morris-Commercial LC van. Combine the styling elements of this with the Trojan packaging and you've got the makings of a J-type!

Right : Still not quite as the production model turned out, this is how the J-type appeared in early publicity.

When a 'Series Y' replacement became necessary, Morris-Commercial had the task of producing it, although Morris carried on their tradition of building car-derived vans with the Series MCV van and pick-up, the Cowley range, based on the Oxford car.

Photographs exist of two different J-type prototypes, one of which shows that the designers developing the J-type had experimented with incorporating the Company's then-current frontal styling into the vehicle. This 'PV'-esque vertical-slatted grille sat rather uncomfortably on the very stylishly curvaceous pressed steel body. Thankfully, this treatment was not approved, and the pear-shaped and horizontally-slatted grille that has become synonymous with the van went through to production.

The J-type ('49 - '57)

The J-type 10 cwt van was provided with a 1476cc, 36 bhp, side valve engine (based on the Morris Oxford car unit) and

Left: Early J-type prototype.

An illustration of a standard steel-bodied J-type drawn with beautiful penmanship for a 'Motor Trader' article. It clearly shows the early rectangular sidelights.

The earliest known J-type for which we have recorded details is OWL 326. This was supplied to The Oxford Co-operative Society and carried chassis number J/R 010. It was first registered on the 17th September, 1949.

Right: The oldest surviving van is believed to be that owned by the Celtic Old Vehicle Owners Club. This, we are told, carries chassis number J/R 485.

3-speed gearbox. The van was advertised as having 150 cu ft of load carrying capacity, mainly because of its radical forward-control packaging. It had 16" wheels, and was fitted with a spiral-bevel rear axle, although after 11,276 vans had been produced this was changed for a hypoid-bevel axle. Chassis numbers, which started at 001, were prefixed by J/R or J/L indicating right- or left-hand drive. Initially vans had cable linkage for the accelerator, but this was soon changed for a rod mechanism. Another difference on early vehicles was the fitting of rectangular sidelights (as fitted to the Austin Atlantic) under the headlamps, rather than the later round ones. At first very few vans were available for the home market.

In June 1954 the engine cowling was revised, the attractive angular hinged item giving way to a more rounded, lift-off one.

In the years following WWll, export sales were vital to the economy. Many J-types were supplied to export markets and were shipped as 'Completely Knocked Down' (C.K.D) kits

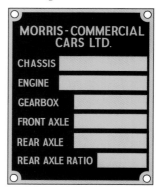

MORRIS-COMMERCIAL CARS LTD.

CHASSIS	
ENGINE	
GEARBOX	
FRONT AXLE	
REAR AXLE	
REAR AXLE RATIO	

The chassis plate of a J-type, which is to be found near to the radiator filler cap inside the cab.

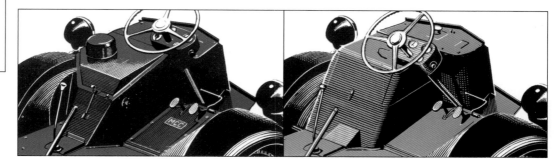

Early (left) and later engine covers.

for assembly at their destination. There are details on J-types having been sold to the following countries: Australia; Bahamas; Belgium; Burma; Canada; Ceylon; Cyprus; Colombia; Denmark; Ireland; Finland; the Gold Coast; Holland; Indonesia; India; Italy; Kenya; Malaysia; Malta; Mexico; New Zealand; Nigeria; Norway; Pakistan; Perak; Rhodesia; South Africa; Sweden; Switzerland and Thailand; although many other countries must also have been targeted by the Nuffield Export staff.

Left-hand drive vans had all mechanical items, engine cowling, steering column etc. moved over to the opposite side, and the two surviving examples have central accelerator pedals!

The J/B and Austin 101 ('57 - '61)

The J-type was updated in 1957, with the fitting of the O.H.V. 1489cc, 42 bhp, 'B' series engine, mated to a 4-speed box, a move which transformed the driving characteristics of the van. The engine

Below: J-types in service with the NRMA (the Australian equivalent of the RAC) at the Melbourne Olympics in 1956. One of these vans has been restored and is used by the NRMA for publicity purposes.

Left: 1955. One of a fleet of J-types supplied to Radio Mexicana. Note the unusual addition of a tubular 'nerf bar' to the bumper.

Left: Fraser & Neave, Malaya's largest brewer and soft drinks manufacturer, took delivery of this finely-lettered van in 1950.

Above: 1954. Mail being delivered to the 'Gothic' at the time of Her Majesty the Queen's visit to Ceylon, by one of at least 19 known to be in their fleet.

Left: A pair of J-types supplied to the Post Office, Nairobi, Kenya in 1950.

Ken Cooke's '58 Austin 101 with owner, in a scene from the popular TV series 'Heartbeat'. XRH 885 was originally registered to Sandersons Paints in Glasgow.

cowling was again revised to accomodate the different engine, the rounded, lift-off cowling being replaced with a bulkier but similarly styled one.

Chassis numbers, starting at 36,266, carried on from the earlier J-type but were now prefixed with JB/MR (B-series/Morris). To distinguish it from its predecessor, the van became known as the Morris-Commercial J/B. Badge-engineering by the British Motor Corporation saw an Austin version of the J/B introduced, known as the Austin 101, which differed from the J/B only in the design of the front grille panel and the badging. These carried chassis numbers in sequence with the J/B but prefixed by JB/AR (B series/Austin) so it is not possible to work out separate production figures for Austin or Morris versions.

With the advent of the Austin version of the van the 'Morris-Commercial' front grille badge gave way to a larger 'Morris' one. Austin versions appear to have been fitted with 15" wheels as standard, whilst the J/B seems to have retained 16" wheels as standard and offered the 15" as an option.

J-type and J/B

101

The chassis plate common to the J/B and 101, located to the right of the radiator filler cap inside the cab.

A comparison of the two styles of grille panel. The J-type and J/B, identical except for the badge, have more chrome, more slots and a greater delicacy in its treatment, stylistically, than the 101.

Production of the JB ceased early in 1961 although vehicles were still being registered as late as December of the same year. The very last van produced carried chassis number 48,621.

Morris replaced the J/B with the J4, which clothed the same engine in a more modern-looking body of all-steel monocoque construction. The J4 was announced at the 1959 Commercial Motor Show, so

Above: The youngest van known to survive is this GPO planner's van. In need of a bit of TLC, it carries chassis number 48582, which makes it 38 away from the very last one!

for more than a year both the 10 cwt J/B and the J4, rated at 10/12 cwt were being manufactured by Morris-Commercial. Although sitting on the same wheelbase as its predecessor, the J4 - due mainly to its driving position being moved even further forward - boasted of 160 cu ft of load-carrying space. It benefited

from independent front suspension, a panoramic one-piece front windscreen, and the option of hinged doors for both driver and passenger was offered - a departure from its predecessor. The change of driving position also allowed the 'M-C' engineers to bring the engine and drivetrain back to the vehicle centreline.

The J4 in turn was developed into the Sherpa, whilst the Morris-Commercial company went from badging their commercials as Morris to BMC and then through many changes of name including Freight Rover, Leyland Daf and ultimately culminating in LDV Ltd., who have two J-types on site at Drews Lane, Birmingham, one of which has been totally restored by apprentices in their Training Department. This thorough restoration saw many new panels being made in the Training workshops, and even included the manufacture of a new set of GPO specification rubber wings!

Left: Two J-types in a display area at LDV's Training Facility at the Drews Lane Plant; a GPO Planner's van, RLB 778 - restored by LDV apprentices, and XMT 899 - a standard van originally owned by the John Lewis Partnership.
The vans are used for promotional purposes these days.

GPO Use – 100 cu ft Mail Van

The major fleet user of the J-type and the J/B was the GPO, who used them as Postal, Utility, Planners, and Radio Investigation vans. 6,147 J-types were bought by the GPO - approximately one in every eight of the vehicles built! The most obvious difference in the specification of these GPO J-types was the fitting of rubber front and rear wings, which required the fitting of the headlamps and sidelights to the cabside, rather than being mounted on castings on the wings as on standard vans. GPO vans had much improved locks for security, with Mail vans also having a rear door locking bar, which could be operated by the driver from inside

the vehicle. Mail vans also had a wooden partition with sliding door to separate the load area from the cab. This door was lockable for obvious security reasons. Some GPO 'J' vans were also fitted with an opening driver's windscreen.

The Post Office, possibly quite arbitrarily, designated these vans as having 100 cu ft carrying capacity, although Morris-Commercial's own advertising suggests a much greater potential volume. It may well be that the manufacturer could include the space alongside the driver, whilst the GPO might only have measured the space within the body secured by the partition.

The GPO also tested a batch of diesel-powered J-types, the remains of one of which survived until recently on a farm near Stoke-on-Trent. It had long since lost its engine to a good cause, but there was enough left to show that it was indeed a diesel, including a petrol cap with 'Fuel oil' pressed into it.

LUU 572, chassis number J/R 4513, the first J-type in GPO service, was registered on 31st of January 1951.
It carried serial number 41308.
Worthy of note are the GR crowns and black ROYAL MAIL lettering.
Subsequent vans had the gold lettering with black drop shadow and yellow highlights on all letters.

Mail vans were a common sight on British roads throughout the '50s and well into the '60s. When sold out of service, the GPO would strip the vehicles of their livery and security locks and sell them on at auction, the princely sum of £25 being the price mentioned as being paid by many subsequent owners!

Nowadays the few survivors are much sought-after with but a handful preserved. Only three have been returned to their original livery so far, but others are known to be undergoing full restoration.

Stores Van

The 10-cwt Stores Carrying Vehicle (Closed), Type 1 (Morris) was introduced 'to improve the economic efficiency of centralised stores delivery pools'.

More or less a combination of both Postal and Utility, the cab was fitted out in line with the Utility, sharing fittings such as the engine cover-mounted folding writing table, passenger seat with battery beneath and padlocked tool compartment adjacent. It was also fitted with a mesh screen between cab and load area, but differed from a Utility in not having any requirement for a second-level floor. Photographs of one example show it to be kitted out with mesh rear window guards, as per Postal vans.

Racking was not specified, but could be fitted if necessary. It was recommended that Minor van fittings were used where suitable.

Fixing holes for a standard pin-type towing clevis were provided in the reinforced rear bumper mounting bar. It was specified that the clevis would only be supplied if the request was authorised by the Area Engineer, and could only be used to tow trailer tool-carts.

GPO Utility, 10 cwt Type 1 (Morris)

This specification was for "use by two-man parties not requiring a ladder longer than a Ladder, Extension, No 5 which was 8' 4" closed 20' 0" extended".

A passenger seat was provided, which could tilt to facilitate access to the vehicle battery. A folding writing table was mounted above the engine cover, which could be raised when access to the engine was required. Vehicle tools were carried in a padlocked compartment adjacent to the battery compartment.

The body was separated from the cab by a fixed wire-mesh screen, providing security for the van's contents. Incorporated in the top portion of this screen, behind the driver, was a two-compartment locker for Engineering Instructions, books, papers and personal effects. The wire-mesh screen also carried two hooks for hats and coats.

Within the body was a second floor, 8" above the standard floor, the space between being divided into two compartments. The off-side area would accomodate the No. 5 Ladder, whilst the nearside would carry such items as digging tools pruning rods and folding steps. The nearside of the main space within the body contained standard rack units, and space was allocated for a Jointers toolbox. The rest of the space available was considered suitable for such items as tent sections (used to cover holes when not filled in immediately), Generator Sets, Portable Pumps and Caution Lamps.

As with the Stores van, fixing holes for a standard pin-type towing clevis were provided in the reinforced rear bumper mounting bar and with the same specification that the clevis would only be supplied if the request was authorised by the Area Engineer, and could only be used to tow trailer tool-carts.

MYF 492, the prototype J Utility, delivered in 1952. Note the king's cypher.

NYH 280, an early side-valve Utility.
Note the rear window security mesh screens, common to Mail Vans and Utilities.

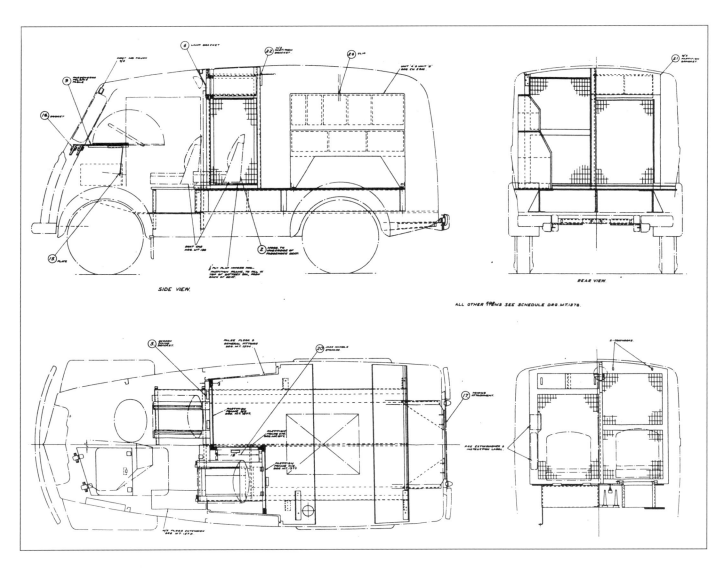

A general arrangement drawing showing the second floor within the rear body, partition, position of standard racks, etc.

Planner's Van

The full title of this version was 'Area Planning and General Purpose Vehicle, Type 1 (Morris). It was designed for "duties requiring transport for three to six men (including the driver)", a mobile field office, or "transport for a cable fault localisation duty for which the provision of a test van is not warranted".

A passenger seat was provided, as well as seats for a further four men along the sides of the body section, split three on the near-side and one on the off-side. These seats could fold back and be secured by leather ties, to improve load space and to allow access to lockers underneath. Also mounted on the off-side within the body of the van was a drop flap type table unit, for the laying out of plans, using light test gear and for writing. The table unit incorporated a pencil groove, as well as deep map pockets and partitioned compartments for forms and instructions. A light was fitted above the table.

As with the Utility, a folding writing table was mounted above the engine cover, which could be raised when access to the engine was required. Vehicle tools were carried in a padlocked compartment adjacent to the battery compartment.

Within the body, a three-section ladder could be carried on the floor of the vehicle, the forward end of the ladder being tucked under the driver's seat. Bulky items of test gear or apparatus could be carried, requiring the folding back of the seats and the lowering of the table top.

Again, fixing holes for a standard pin-type towing clevis were provided, and, as with the Stores van and Utility, accompanied by the proviso regarding authorisation by the Area Engineer, and for trailer tool-cart towing only.

A very rare sight indeed, a brace of restored planning vans. Nearest to the camera is RLB 778, restored in the Training workshops at LDV; alongside is 949 BYY owned by Ray Kings.

R. I. Van

The full title of this version was 'Area Radio Investigation Vehicle, Type 1 (Morris)'. It was designed for use on "Radio Investigation duties where the Minor van, modified for such work, was inadequate".

A passenger seat with tool-storage locker underneath, was provided, as well as a bench seat for a further two men on the near-side of the body section, although primarily provided for the use of a man operating equipment within the body. This bench seat could fold back and be secured against the side of the van, to allow access to lockers underneath and to improve access to equipment carried. As with the Utility, a folding writing table was mounted above the engine cover.

A mesh security screen separated the body from the cab area, enabling the body to be locked without restricting access to the cab. A door was incorporated, giving access to the body from the cab. A hinged area in the screen allowed for the carrying of a ladder.

Within the body, a three-compartment apparatus locker was mounted above the ladder space. This had

three sliding panels in the top for access. These panels could also be used to mount and set out equipment for making tests from within the vehicle.

A rotatable aerial-mast with coaxial connector box was located towards the rear of the body. This was controlled remotely by a handle to the rear of the driver's seat. An additional business radio aerial could be fitted centrally on the roof, if required. Power for the test apparatus came from a 5 amp point wired to the vehicle battery. Additional capacity could be obtained by the use of additional 6V car-type batteries stowed within the body of the vehicle.

100 cu. ft. Mail Van and Utility in tandem. YLH 859, owned by Colin Ellis, clearly shows its inner partition. The Utility is owned by Chris Bowkett.

These two shots were taken, moments apart, on the 14th of November, 1962,
by bus enthusiast Mike Sutcliffe.
He was obviously interested in the London Transport RT, but for us it is the other
vehicles that grab our attention. Both J-types in shot are GPO vans, the YLH
registered one on the left sporting Royal Mail lettering on its grille panel.

Specialised Applications

Right: A very boxy van; with its flat sides it seems more like a small PV . Surprisingly, this vehicle also has a flat front with a single piece screen, which would appear to have involved a major rework of the grille panel supplied!

Morris-Commercial were happy to supply the chassis to coachbuilders, in two forms - chassis with grille panel supplied loose, and chassis with assembled front end complete with windshield and quarter lights plus front wheelarches and wings. A significant number of J-type, J/B and 101 chassis were supplied in this way, allowing coachbuilders to offer unique bodies to the customer's own special requirements. Configurations known to have been produced include luton vans, pick-ups (including tippers), ice cream vans, milkfloats and mobile libraries.

Right: A nicely proportioned builders truck with dropside body. The cab, whilst being totally coachbuilt, incorporates the standard wings and headlamp arrangement.

With Austin Crompton Parkinson Electric Vehicles Limited being part of the Nuffield empire, Morris-Commercial even experimented with an electric J-type and one is believed to have entered service as a milkfloat with a dairy in Solihull.

Right: A gown van with beautifully finished coachwork. Again quite 'PV'-esque, its slab-sides are relieved by the careful use of mouldings in flowing curves. An accomplished piece of coachbuilding.

Above: A restored coachbuilt vehicle, owned by Fred Bell, that used the chassis with grille panel.

> *If the standard body is not suitable for your type of business, why not have a special body built onto a J/B chassis? Suitably painted, the van will act as your constant ambassador to the public - your customers. Your transport and maintenance staff will take pride in these smart-looking J/B vans. They will work with more care on a vehicle of which they are proud, to the benefit of the vehicle.*

This brochure illustration shows what the company supplied as the 'chassis with assembled front end complete with windshield and quarter lights plus front wheelarches and wings'

Above: A high-roofed van, with the Capon fleet, shows how a standard steel-bodied van could be successfully adapted by a talented coachbuilder to create unique bodywork.

Left: The earliest known example of a J-type pick-up is this one exhibited at the Limerick Show in 1950. W F Poole, the Morris-Commercial Distributors for Eire, had this nicely-proportioned Irish-bodied example as part of their display.

The standard steel-bodied J-type was frequently converted for ambulance and minibus use. Martin-Walter, Wadhams and Frank Grounds, amongst others, supplied many similar vehicles.

Left: This conversion was carried out by Martin-Walter.

A Unique Coachbuilt GPO Van – A Real One-Off!

PGO 2, first registered in July 1954, appears in GPO official records as a Radio Investigation van, although these same records show that it was not part of a batch of J-types bought with this use in mind.

The photograph below shows that it was indeed a one-off coachbuilt J-type built on a 'chassis with assembled front end complete with windshield and

quarter lights'. The bodywork closely follows the shape of a standard steel-bodied J-type, and may well be entirely of wood construction (which was a perfectly commonplace method used widely by manufacturers and coachbuilders of the period) with a fabric covering to the roof. A wooden body could indicate an attempt to

provide a covert investigation facility. The choice of an internal aerial, and there seems to be no provision for anything linking to an external aerial in the photograph of the interior, would preclude the use of a standard steel-bodied van, the metal panels of which would create a 'Faraday's Cage' effect where much of the radio signal would be attenuated.

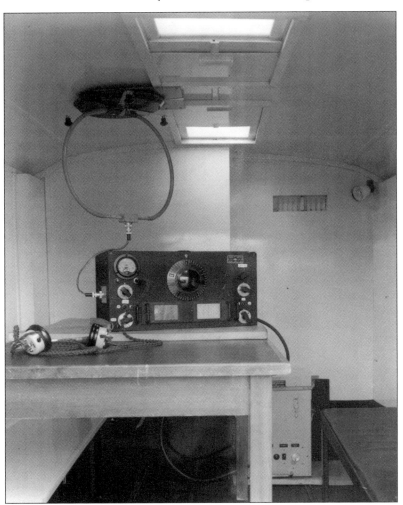

Two opening rooflights allowed ventilation within the sparely equipped body, which has no access to or from the cab area. To standard GPO specifications are the rubber wings (the exterior shot showing how shiny and well-finished these items were when brand new) and two windscreen wipers.

This van was given the serial number 17110 and was later re-registered 461 DJJ. No subsequent history is known.

I doubt whether we will find out more as to why this remained as a one-off, or how and why the decision was made to follow the route whereby the subsequent R. I. Vans positively bristled with external aeriels.

Ice Cream Vans

The J-type was a delight for the Ice Cream trade. Its size and forward control layout made it ideal for use as an Ice Cream van. Occasionally the bodywork of the standard van was adapted by fitting large windows with opening serving hatches, and usually - but not always - by raising the roof to give more headroom inside. More often a chassis or chassis plus cab front would have a body built especially for it by one of the many coachbuilders specialising in this field. Consequently many varied body styles can be seen on the Ice Cream vans that survive.

Whitby Engineering of Crewe, Europe's largest manufacturer of Mobile Sales vehicles, have three J-types in their Heritage Collection of preserved Ice Cream vans. Two are in excellent restored condition, **YHT 511** and **3315 NA**, whilst another awaits the moment that a busy schedule allows for some remedial work to be carried out on it. The two photographs show the vans at a Music Live event in Birmingham in 2000.

Granelli's of Macclesfield have a J-type, **TMB 337,** which they have owned from new. It was purchased in 1953 as a chassis/grille panel and was fitted with a coachbuilt body by Winards of Wigan. Upon completion it was registered in September 1954. After 15 years of service it was retired and restored in 1994.

LDK 528

This van, restored to its original livery by Graham Wilton, was first registered in 1954. It is one of three vans found parked up behind the premises of Johnnie's Ices in Stalybridge. Much Painstaking detective

work brought to light this photo of the van when new, and enabled Graham to retain the original registration number.

EVG 79

It had long been Gary Sutton's ambition to own this particular Ice Cream van, the one most beloved of its owner Stanley Driver, known as Bunshi, whom Gary had known for many years.

Gary, who has modern ice cream vans as well as a couple of restored Bedford CAs, had already carried out the restoration of YHT 511, which previously worked with Verrecchia's of

Bristol. EVG had somehow become separated from Mr. Driver following use in some film work.

Its documents changed hands a couple of times, and for a while it worked for its living, selling ice cream with Carter's Steam Fair. Then came a 'phonecall from the owner saying that it had been vandalised and did I know someone who might be able to give it a good home as well as the necessary care and attention required to return it to its former glory.

The archive photo (inset) shows that EVG 79 was first used by Aldous of Norwich, although most of its working life was with Bumshi's/Bunshi's. Above: The finished restoration, a fine tribute to Stanley Driver.

Above: EVG 79 at work with Carter's Steam Fair.

Above: As towed to its new home. It does not look too bad, but removal of the outer panels brought to light a very fragile body frame. In this shot it can be seen that there is damage at the base of the B-pillar

EVG 79 - the restoration.

The easy part was putting them in touch with Gary! In his capable hands, EVG underwent a thorough restoration. I had no idea that the ice cream van would be so comprehensively stripped during its rebuild. It had, after all, been working fairly recently.

The aluminium side panels were removed in order to gain access to the ash frame, much of which needed replacing. There were times, I'm sure, when Gary thought it would never go back together again! But gradually and methodically things got done; a new floor, new front panelling and woodwork, new side panelling, new rear door frames and the van started to look something like how it originally did when it left the Kennings coachworks.

This has turned out so well that Gary's thoughts are turning towards trying to find its sister vehicle in the Bunshi fleet, JVG 72. What are the chances of locating it? Pretty remote, I'd say. It has got to be worth a try though!

Below: Not much of the frame left after removal of all that needs replacing! A lot of the wooden floor structure had to be redone also.

Shots at various stages during the restoration show just how thoroughly the job was carried out.

Right: JVG 72, a 1956 van, was last heard of sold at auction to a woman in Canterbury who was going to drag it into her garden..........
.... and use it as a greenhouse!

Below: SPW 310, a 1955 J-type, working at Bressingham in 1974. Nothing is known as to the fate of this van or its whereabouts .

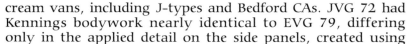

Bunshi's Ices had an interesting fleet of ice cream vans, including J-types and Bedford CAs. JVG 72 had Kennings bodywork nearly identical to EVG 79, differing only in the applied detail on the side panels, created using standard section aluminium mouldings. These Kennings conversions had totally coachbuilt bodies - only the grille panel and front wings are the same as a standard van. Other J-types in the Bunshi fleet were quite different, SPW 310 being coachbuilt but using a complete steel cab-front, whilst ECL 615, also ex-Bunshi, is a conversion of a standard steel body, retaining both steel rear doors and with serving hatches incorporated into the standard body side panels.

Above: First registered in 1950, ECL 615 is seen on the move near Crawley in 1983. ECL still appears occasionally at rallies.

Above: SPW 310 and JVG 72, in the company of CAs from the Bunshi fleet. It can be seen in this photograph from 1974 that the company had vans lettered up as both 'Bumshi' and 'Bunshi', the latter being brought in at the insistence of the local Council, so as not to offend the sensibilities of the locals. Unbelievable!

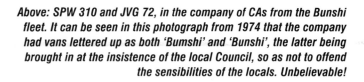

Kennings were a major supplier of ice cream vans, which they featured prominently in their advertising at the time. It is interesting to follow the development of their ads, from line drawing through illustration to photograph of an actual van supplied to Hulley's Dairy, of Ecclesfield.

The photograph below shows a batch of four Kennings vans about to be delivered to their fortunate owners, James Akers of Belper, Levaggi's of Denton, West View Dairies and, we think, A Morris of Somercotes.

Left: Whilst working with Carter's Steam Fair EVG actually appeared, in colour, in an edition of Playdays magazine. This spin-off from the children's TV programme showed Wobble, a character from the show, taking in the atmosphere.

Right: By 1954 Kennings were also offering the same style of body as a Mobile Library, the only major change being the replacement of the offside serving hatch with shelving and display units.

Agatha is a unique van, rather a rare beast, once home to a host of African insects from scorpions to baboon spiders (early morning renovations needed to be started warily)! Here's her story.

Across Africa in a vest!*

by Richard Maclaurin

In 1983 Sue and I, with our two daughters of six and eight, were finding the UK a bit cramped. Thatcher's reign of grass-roots abuse and financial greed had taken off and Africa's wildlife beckoned.

We cashed in the mortgaged rooms and the Morris 1000, bought a tent and tickets - presto, sun instead of rain. Work to be had mining, and Sue teaching in a local Zimbabwean school, we were rolling.

The Rhodesian/Zimbabwe war had just ended and a mixture of euphoria, excitement and friendship was in the air. The killing had stopped, and the local ex-terrorists or freedom fighters were centred in a new light industrial site in Gweru. Passing the entrance in my rebuilt Isuzu pick-up, a 1965 model, I spied, in the distance, what looked like a Post Office van.

I immediately drove to the far end of the yard. The poor old van had the back chopped out, and was in a sorry state. No floors, and started with a cough, belching blue smoke to a selection of rattles and knocks.

Saved from the axe - Gweru 1983

I could feel
a sense of nervousness........

By now, the owner and I were surrounded by a throng of lads, fresh from the bush, whose only sight of a white male had been as a hated enemy at whose hands many of their mates had died. I could feel a sense of nervousness creeping up on me, as I stared at this dilapidated old J-type. It was to be used to ferry ox-carts to and from the outlying villages, apparently. Fat chance, I thought.

"Did I wish to sell my Isuzu?" the Matabele gent asked. And this stupid voice piped up from nowhere "Yes mate, I'll do a straight swap. I'll have your van, you take the Isuzu."

All smiles now, the locals pressed round me, knowing they'd acquired, out of the blue, a virtually new diesel pickup, for an old heap, from a mentally sick white fool. Excellent.

Sue and the family named her Agatha, and we took her to bits. The engine was rebuilt, using mix and match - new bearings, shells, pistons and rings I think from Japan, Mazda. I remember the gleaming new metal of the rebore. The new pistons fitted perfectly, but a little

Text and Illustrations © Richard Maclaurin

*Richard's suggestions for a title included:

"Idiot in drawers"
"The leather beard"
and
"A life with sheep"
which made
"J-type endurance"
(his attempt at a sensible one)
seem just too mundane by comparison!

short on the skirt. The new clutch from the MO Morris club back here in the UK. And points.

The radiator recored, I cobbled together the back-end using timber and sheet galvanised tin, and made a tailboard from timber. A new floor I think, and a repaint - the olive green made up from whatever enamel I could find out in the bush workshop and sheds where we lived. I particularly liked the discovery of the chained clutch mechanism when I first stripped her - a perfect design - non-stretch, a dab of grease and never wears, easy to replace.

New springs and track rod ends. Incidentally, under the Zimbabwean number

Did you say you needed the van tomorrow? There's a slight problem......

plate, (on the back, I think), was an original UK number plate, faded and worn, so the vehicle I suspect was taken out to Rhodesia probably by its then owner, in the late fifties or early sixties, after early years in Britain. Perhaps a carpenter, engineer or builder, all needed back in those days in the Colonies.

Slowly Agatha became mobile, bobbing about the hot and dusty dirt roads, ferrying our two kids, by now aged eight and ten, to school.

Dusty and spattered, struggling over rough ground, she carried the materials with which we built our dairy and refrigerated coolers; the cement blocks and gum tree poles, the roofing sheets and cement. The milk churns in their turn were loaded and carried over the three miles of bush tracks and five miles of hot tarmac to the factory. The 5.30 am start, queueing in the hot sun, returning by 7.30 loaded again with udder creams and sterilization fluids, empty churns, one hundredweight sacks of cow feed... and footsore travellers. Once, blowing out a

rear tyre, overloaded, panic at the rifle shot - slewing along sideways creeping home on the rim, the spare, of course, flat. The rubber blocks wired between the springs and chassis saved the rear springs.

I nearly burnt her completely, once - the oxygen and acetylene stood in the back as I welded up railway lines to form cow stalls in the dairy. The grass had lit, but was invisible in the heat of midday - we'd had three years of drought. The next thing, Agatha is smelling hot and, leaving the cutting torch roaring on a concrete block, it was a sprint through flames, desperate start and away, dragging torch hastily behind us, out onto the sandy track and safety. It might have been a big bang and goodbye Agatha et al.

I remember, too, baboons raiding the hen house, two hundred yards from the dairy, and having to drive furiously - shooting at them with the Mauser. Big holes through the hen house, clouds of chickens, with happy egg-clutching baboons bounding off into the kopjes - yes, a J-type suits the western riding approach, but remember to open the doors first!

Petrol was often unavailable, so we bought drums of TVO Power Paraffin and drums of methanol. A 50/50 mix

Nothing in the workshop manual about this....
Hmmm.....

provided the usual performance, if a little sooty. However, a spate of dirt road ambushing developed. As neither power nor speed was available as ambush escape, I wondered how to best protect Sue and the two girls on their school runs. Unlikely as it was she'd be ambushed (they'd be too busy falling about laughing) I did raise the methanol to 70%. The J-type became a throbbing beast, 0-60mph was managed within a day, white heat pouring from the cylinder head. The test run proved that Sue could accelerate out of harm. Luckily the ambushes ceased, and so Agatha's pistons and valves survived the inevitable metallic liquefaction that was pending should 'wellying' on methanol have been required. But that Santa Pod experience in a J-type was unexpected and exciting.

We'd only been in Zimbabwe four years and Mugabe chopped the milk price, leaving us broke. It was illegal to export vehicles for profit but we were determined to hang on to Agatha. I don't think she could have been saved if I'd stayed any longer - for instance it was only the next month that our neighbour was shot, and they came in the night for us too. Not much fun for our two girls, but we'd mixed and worked with our black neighbours, Agatha helping them and us - so the terrorists laid off. I had

to drive her through the bush a lot, often armed up - but we didn't fit steel plate and industrial nylon belting inside Agatha, as many did to their vehicles in case of attack, because it would have damaged the bodywork and the weight would have broken the springs.

Our farm was burnt out by bush fires and so we went on the road. Agatha provided a sound home as we travelled and searched for a new start. Camping and living out of the back was a fine bush experience, the girls slept inside and we outside. As I had worked with wildlife in the UK, we prepared to journey north from Bulawayo, the 150 miles to Whange game reserve, for a job interview. This road ran through 80 miles of thick bush, encroaching on the road.

There continued many terrorist attacks along this stretch, and so vehicles gathered each morning and, with an armed escort vehicle, sped north flat out. A J-type would never keep up, so we left early trundling slowly onwards alone, the girls lying flat in the rear of the van. Tension mounted as we passed a burning lorry, then a burnt out bus, and then the armed convoy zoomed past.

A brew up was the only counter-insurgency that we practiced, and so we pulled off the road and enjoyed our tea, the noise of the cicadas easing the

Sue's school run.....

The J-type became a throbbing beast....

stillness. Of course Agatha started up and drove on ok - a mile down the road we came upon an army pick-up, jittery soldiers, radiator steaming. No oil! We glugged our spare gallon into their sump, refilled the rad, and they roared off - weapons sprouting from windows.

Memories, too, of belligerent and suspicious checkpoint soldiers at road blocks, confused by this antique van. "Why weren't we in the convoy?" "Where had we been?" "What had we seen?" "Why were we in this old van?" "How had it driven so far?" and so on.

I couldn't really explain to them about the reliability of a Morris-Commercial and the principles of dependable, if slow, transport, or that we lived in it, or how brewing up is more satisfying than war. And I didn't get the job, so we stayed and enjoyed the wildlife, before the final journey from Africa for Agatha.

The government was Shona, the opposition were Matabele - we drove the long way down to Bulawayo (Matabeleland) over a huge dusty plain

Overdid the spring assisters, maybe.......

on an empty road, the doors open, Sue following in her 1959 Mercedes. The Matabele exporters gave us a licence to take out the J-type as 'domestic goods' - anyway who would sell her for profit? A joke. Mad white people. And the Mercedes, a perfectly solid '190', cream colour, we gave to friends who now display her in South African rallies. A beautiful car.

That last African journey was fun. We had some books, our tools and a milk churn in the back containing clothes - all our worldly possessions. The roads were empty - the early start with rising mists over seventy miles of Somabula Flats, a great rolling plain dotted with gum and thorn tree groves, rocky outcrops, distant blue hills and rippling heat.

Agatha drove steadily onwards, the empty road to ourselves, the huge sky, the spanners tinkling against the milk churn behind me. We stopped in the shade of thorn trees to picnic and brew up, the J-type

In a J-type one can lie full length over the seats with feet waving out one side and head the other, whilst steering and accelerating by hand. Blows away the heat and the red Zimbabwean dust.

cooling and creaking. Ever onward to Bulawayo, down through hotter scrub and scattered bush, sand, quartz, the ramshackle suburbs and shipping agents yard - to finally park her up in a cool shed backing onto the railway line, her goods wagon to Durban and return home.

Somabula Flats

Loaded onto an open flatbed, the steam train carried Agatha south across the border into South Africa and Durban Docks. Driven into a container and swung aboard ship, the next two weeks at sea to finally unload at Southampton docks. Back home and soot stained! It had cost us a little under £2000 to ferry her over, and we had our £40 allowance as we flew out of Africa, with which we collected her, filled up the tank, and drove up to Kent, her bright yellow Zimbabwe number plates an invitation to motorway police. No papers and covered in Bulawayo dust!

Returning to the UK in 1984 meant new work for Agatha. Our few possessions in the back were soon replaced with roofing and building tools, slates, tiles and cement. No, it was too much.... not fair on such a vehicle. I'd bought a WW2 Dodge ambulance which carried massive loads, and so Agatha was ready for new horizons - advertised to go to an enthusiast only. Bob Sandford happily took her away.

The Scammells, the Austins, the Morrises, the AEC Matador, Riley, and Rover that followed could never fill her place, her unique open-door excellence and cheery progress across the world against any odds. *It really had been touch and go getting her out of that yard in Gweru!*

And, once again, Zimbabwe has declined into destruction and anarchy, my African friends reduced to disease and poverty.

The madness of dictatorship!

and my other favourite too! A Scammell Pioneer R100 Tractor

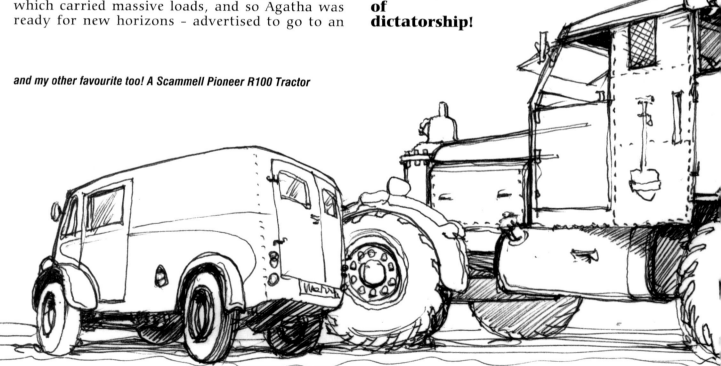

I had wanted a J-type van to use in connection with my business, and had been looking for some time.

On to Doctor Bob....

A postscript by Bob Sandford

Eventually, in the 6/80 and MO Club newsletter (Summer 1985) an advert appeared for a J-type which had been brought back from Zimbabwe, the owner (Richard Maclaurin) having returned to this country.

Having made the necessary telephone calls, Linda and I set off on Sunday afternoon to Richard's farm at Doddington in Kent to look the van over, and to my surprise it was virtually rust free, but looked a bit odd as the body had been altered. Having completed a deal, we returned home to make the necessary arrangements to transport the van back to my workshop.

Thursday evening my colleague Barry and I, armed with a set of trade plates, set off in my A60 Van with the intention of driving Agatha back. Would it start or wouldn't it? We took with us a set of points, plugs, oil, water, petrol and tow rope, and had just passed through Rochester, when we suddenly remembered - we had left the battery behind. Too late to turn back now, so we made a quick diversion to buy a new one. Not a very promising start to the evening.

Three photos of the van taken whilst in Zimbabwe.
The old chap, Kamba, worked with the Maclaurins on anything from mechanical matters to milking their cows!
The shot on the right shows just how much the van was taken apart during its rebuild, and also shows the Zimbabwe registration, 333 - 725T

was getting dark, so we hitched up the tow rope and off we went. After about a mile we managed to tow start the van, and this time it carried on running. As the headlights refused to work, and the brakes were awful, we decided to leave the tow rope hitched up, but drive Agatha back under her own steam to lessen the load on the A60.

A very interesting drive home, especially on descending Chatham Hill where Agatha flatly refused to slow down! With roadworks at the bottom of the hill, governed by traffic lights (which were, of course, on red) panic set in. Miraculously, at the last moment the lights changed to green. Negotiating the roadworks at breakneck speed, we carried on to Erith. (White knuckle rides at Thorpe Park are for cissies).

Back at the workshop by about 10.15pm, we parked Agatha in the yard, then on to the pub for a quick pint to calm the nerves. Next day, on inspecting the van, I discovered that the body had been lengthened by about ten inches, the roof and top half having been cut and moved back. Windows had been cut in, and a panel had been cut out of the roof. The lower half had been chopped off where the rear door hinges would normally bolt to, and metal had been 'pop riveted' on to make it longer. Several

We arrived at Doddington around 7pm and set about getting Agatha started. Fitting a new set of points and connecting the battery we cranked the engine. Lo' and behold it started first time, ran for about three minutes and then stopped. No amount of effort could get it started again. By this time it

The original advert indicates Richard's desire that the van finds a good home. It certainly did!

MORRIS COMMERCIAL JB Van : 195? in black.   This advertisement is for the JB brought home from Zimbabwe by Dick Maclaurin, MJ/446. Whilst Dick would be very sorry to part with the van, he feels that 'Agatha' would be better off with some kind person to restore her, as it is likely to be some time before he gets around to it, and she is sitting in the open. A van with a unique history, it would be a pity to see her deteriorate beyond help, whereas at the present time she is eminently restorable. Will anyone who is interested please contact Dick, who is not asking a lot for her, as he has her welfare at heart. Number to ring is: 079 586 233. (Kent)

Doctor Bob's ambition was to own a standard van, so much work had to be carried out to bring Agatha back to its original specification.

yards of angle iron had been welded on the inside along the swage line, to strengthen the body and to form the window frames. A wooden tailgate had been fitted instead of rear doors.

I decided to remove all of the extra metal and the roof to see exactly what remained. I now had to make a decision as to what to do with it. The easiest way would have been to make it into a pick-up, but no, I had wanted a panel van, and a panel van it would be.

A quick visit to fellow 'J' enthusiast Chris Bowkett, with camera in hand to take some photos of RGK, confirmed how the body should look. Chris also offered me a pair of rear doors which needed considerable welding but were essential to the restoration, as I needed a reference point to weld the roof and upper body back on. Many hours were then spent manufacturing panels and welding these in place. Eventually it started to look like a J-type should.

All the mechanical bits were in good condition, as the engine had been rebuilt in Zimbabwe. The brakes needed a complete overhaul, the kingpins were well past their best, and the front axle needed reaming and bushing where the kingpins fit. Strangest of all, there were no front shock absorbers fitted. With all this done and the body finished and painted, it was off to the MOT station for the test.

Armed with a new MOT and the necessary paperwork, the next stop was the VRO at Sidcup, where Agatha was duly registered as OSU 787. First put to work at the Enfield Pageant of Motoring in 1989, Agatha spent the next ten years happily transporting spares to the various classic car shows, gaining much admiration.

Footnote:
It would be true to say that had Agatha been resident in this country all of her life, with the normal amount of rust associated with J-types, it would have been unrealistic as a restoration project and would, quite probably, have been broken for spares.

....and beyond!

After many years of use around the rallies - carrying his autojumble - Bob found that it was too small for his needs. Rather than see it gradually fall into disrepair, Bob sold it on to fellow enthusiast Sean Carrara.

Far left. The van in Bob's workshop, looking very much like a standard van again.

Left. OSU 787, now with Sean Carrara. I'm sure that the Maclaurins will be pleased to see that the van is still carrying the name Agatha after all these years.

Postal J-type Memories

by
Don Foster

My driver training began in November 1963, at which time I was a postman at the Battersea District Post Office on Lavender Hill, London SW11, close to the large rail station of Clapham Junction.

Along with two other aspiring drivers I embarked upon a fortnight of instruction using J-type MLH 899 which was one of the older examples fitted with a 3-speed gearbox. No synchromesh so, of course, there was much grating of gears in our inexperienced hands. The usual routine was that our instructor, based at the Kidbrooke GPO workshops, would drive over from there to collect us. At first he, and later one of us, would drive the van along the busy South Circular Road to our area of operations. It seems hard to believe in these days of seat belts, airbags and legislation that then, the two trainees not actually driving sat

MLH 899, Don's first J-type drive! These two shots were taken at Woolwich, London, in November 1963. It is interesting to see a 40"x10" poster pasted directly onto the van's bodywork (quite a common occurrence), even though it is equipped with posterboard brackets!

in the back of the van on ordinary folding wooden chairs with no form of anchorage or restraint. We couldn't have been too bad as I cannot recall anybody ever being tipped off a chair.

My very first attempt at driving was around the internal road system of Kidbrooke workshops, very gingerly to start with. There the three of us could take turns to drive around, encouraging each other while our tutor watched from some distance away as he chatted with his mates. Having grasped the basics we progressed onto the road system of an as yet unbuilt factory estate close to Woolwich Arsenal, a tailor-made training ground.

By the end of the third day it was my turn to be unleashed into the London rush hour traffic for the drive back to Lavender Hill - sink or swim! It was certainly a case of being thrown in at the deep end. All three of us seemed to cope surprisingly well, no doubt being protected to a degree by the 'L' plates.

Having completed the initial two week training period there followed a long spell of what was known as 'confidence driving'. This consisted of two hours each

morning under the eye of a qualified driver. Any van that was available was used for this purpose, all types that are nowadays only seen at rallies.

The quality of driver instruction varied greatly. Most drivers would be content to merely settle down and suggest a drive to a handy transport cafe on the Kingston Bypass. Only one really took the trouble to sort out any problems, a veteran named Joe Conway who had me doing three point turns and reversing around corners until I had mastered these to his satisfaction.

With the regular driving examiner being off with 'flu for a long period, the training went on for quite a long time and it was January 1964 before a substitute examiner was found. The three of us made our way to the GPO workshops on Spanish Road, Wandsworth, for our driving test which was conducted in a decrepit J-type - OYF 542 - which had spent some time standing out of use in the yard. On this morning it was covered in frost and we were to find that some things such as the horn did not work. Despite this I passed the test, though my two companions failed and gave up the idea of being Post Office drivers.

Taking up driving duties, I was allocated to a three man 'set' in which the shifts involved were an early driving week (8.10am to 4.00pm), a late driving week (3.47pm to 10.30pm), with the third week on walking duty. The vehicle for the driving shifts was a

unleashed into the
London rush hour
traffic.........

J/B, 635 BXE, one of the later examples which had the luxury of a 4-speed syncromesh 'box but was still fitted with the old semaphore arm indicators, rather than the then fairly recent innovation of flashing light indicators. On the debit side with this particular van was a tendency for the starter motor to stick, leading to it having to be put in a high gear and rocked to and fro to free it. Another fault at times was that the engine cover, inside the cab, would suddenly become detached and the cab would be filled with a blast of heat and noise. It also had rubber wings which if leaned upon would give way depositing the unwary onto the floor!

In 1964 the smaller vehicles in the Battersea fleet were exclusively J-types of varying age. From memory I can recall elderly LUU 587 and LUU 605, which led a quiet life being used around the SW11 - SW20 area to collect the coin boxes from telephone kiosks. Others were NXO 224, RGK 76, UXV 385, UXV 388, UXV 391, and the quartet of J/Bs - 635 BXE, 694 BXE, 710 BXE and 716 BXE - which had moved on from their original home in Cardiff to the rather different surroundings of South West London.

There were no local fleet numbers and the vans were known by their serial numbers. The four J/Bs, for example, were always referred to as 65157, 65216, 65232 and 65238. I don't think this would be very practical in these days of 7-digit serial numbers!

Of all the J-types 716 BXE was the fleet 'showpiece' usually kept in spotless condition even to the extent of polishing inside the engine compartment. This was normally only permitted

..... even to the extent of polishing inside the engine compartment.

to be driven by two nominated drivers - one of whom was the Driver's Union rep. Anybody else had to obtain the express permission of the Inspector to drive this one!

635 BXE had a working day spanning over 14 hours, 6 days a week. The range of work covered parcel delivery, four collections and two evening express delivery runs. Three 50 minute slots per week were allocated to cleaning and servicing. On cleaning mornings I would take in some 'Turtle Wax' liquid polish to shine up the front of the van and a rag to buff up the black paint on the wheels. I would also keep the cream coloured interior paintwork as clean as possible. Trying to grease the steering with a grease gun was no joke and some drivers tended to neglect this job. Stiff steering on some vans was commonplace.

635 BXE a J/B that was Don's first regular van

The main job of the morning was the High Street parcel delivery from 9am to noon. This covered a wide area around Battersea Park, Battersea Bridge Road, many small streets and firms alongside the River Thames. There were a couple of houseboats where one had to literally 'walk the plank' to get on board.

It was a constant race against the clock as the number of parcels varied with the time of year. Summer would see lots of small rough wooden boxes from Great Yarmouth containing fresh kippers; Christmas would bring turkeys with just a label round the neck. On one occasion I had a large salmon which slid from its wrapping and flopped onto the floor.

By 1966 the emphasis was on mail order parcels. With the advent of a number of multi-storey tower blocks there was a flood of parcels containing curtains and other furnishings from catalogues as people moved in.

The evening period from 7pm to 10.30 pm was interesting as we did two runs to deliver 'express' items which in those days cost one shilling in addition to the normal 4$\frac{1}{2}$d postage rate, for a letter.

I would cover the SW11, 12, 16, 17, and 18 area in 635 BXE, while another driver, in 710 BXE, took care of the areas SW13, 14, 15, 19 and 20. The number of items could vary greatly and the ruling was that inland posted items got priority and all had to be cleared; incoming foreign post was done on the basis of 'as many as possible' but usually, unless there were unusually large numbers of foreign items, it was a point of honour to clear the lot. Some calls were regular, such as the small parcel of catfood which came from a large London store to go to an address in Putney most evenings. An absolute essential was possession of an 'A to Z' London Street Guide to look up locations and plan each run out.

Technically we were supposed to knock and wait for an answer but even in those days many people were loth to open the door at night; calling through the letterbox that you were the postman would often be greeted with disbelief at around 10'o'clock in the evening. There was at least one instance of a driver being asked by the Police what he was up to at that hour.

635 BXE (65157) at Sparkford House Battersea London SW 11, in 1966, on High Street Parcels delivery. Sparkford House was one of a pair of 22 storey tower blocks of 88 flats which had just been opened and which were attracting a large number of mail order parcels.

It was a constant race against the clock.....

In practice what usually happened was that it was better to put the item through the letterbox, ring the bell or bang on the door knocker and take off for the next call while the hall lights were coming on. This avoided the performance of "who is it?" and "what, at this time of night?" This service must have been hopelessly uneconomic as, on some evenings, a fair number of miles were covered in an area extending out to the fringes of Croyden. There was no income from items posted abroad, of course, as the country of origin pocketed this.

A little variety was had on Saturday afternoons when we crossed the Thames and called at the South West District office at Victoria, to collect whatever express items were on hand. Entry to this building was by a tunnel leading to a small loading platform and then back out by another tunnel.

By 1965 interlopers began to appear in the shape of J4 diesels. The first of the quartet of J/Bs to go was 694 BXE, which emerged from a side road and went straight under a large lorry. I well remember the shock of going into Spanish Road workshops and seeing the

twisted heap of wreckage - the only recognisable part was the numberplate. The driver, Ted, who was what is politely known as 'accident prone', escaped, by some miracle, with no more than a cut finger. In a previous accident he had been in a J-type which overturned after colliding with a car. The car was burnt out and Ted emerged, unscathed, through the rear doors of the van while the rescue services were searching for his body.

I went on to become a postman higher grade in mid 1966 and thus parted company with 635 BXE. The three remaining J/Bs were replaced in June and July 1967 by J4 diesels, NYX 305, 306 and 365E. One ironic note was that the much polished 716 BXE came down in the world somewhat, as a few months later I saw it being driven along by Clapham Common. By now it had become a humble mobile greengrocers shop!

Don went on to drive many other Morris-Commercials including J4 diesels, Morris Minors and LD vans.

Text and photographs © Don Foster

In Auspicious Company

No-one has yet been able to tell me the circumstances in which these three icons of the post-war car industry came to be together, but meet up they did!

The Rover T3, four wheel-drive and gas turbine power in a stylish, one-off GRP body, poses in front of Bluebird, Donald Campbell's Proteus jet engine-powered World Land Speed Record car. Humble 4 cylinder-powered J-type owned by Lucas Ltd. brings up the rear.

344 CNM –
Nigel Stanley's Classic Custom Commercial

Seeing this van and admiring Nigel's achievement took me back to my youth. As a callow 14 year old I started buying american custom car magazines. 'Rod and Custom' carried pages of styling sketches by Harry Bradley and Tom Daniels that were particularly inspiring. I spent much time dreaming about how cool customs could be! Around this time rodders on the american scene started getting into customising vans, '32 Sedan Deliveries, split-screen VWs, and the occasional modified Ford Econoline would appear in my favourite reading at the time. A short while later, at Art College in 1967, I first told someone that one of my ambitions was to own a J-type van, and to turn it into something special.

It took nearly twenty years to achieve the 'owning' part of this ambition, by which time advancing years, maturity, call it what you will, really meant that I knew I just could not take a cutting torch

to something so wonderful. I became happy in the knowledge that I owned a pretty well 'stock' example of a JB. Along the way I did see advertised, in the late '80s, a customised J in Northampton, and, given that I drove past there regularly, I found an excuse to go and see whether it was worth making an offer for. Foolishly, I forgot to take a camera with me......

This van had had its door apertures made wider so that the doors (the original steel sliding doors) could be hinged to operate in gull-wing fashion. Really, I kid you not! I couldn't see them in operation, mind you, as the van was parked between the house and a fence and was not movable at that time. The owner must have pushed it into position and got out through the back doors...... I had a good look round it and soon realised that it needed someone much braver and more knowledgeable than me to take it on. Powered by a mid-mounted and very large american V8, where you'd normally expect any load to be, this was coupled up to an independent rear axle setup from a Jaguar, which rolled on mag wheels shod with huge slick tyres. Because the axle had not been set up properly both wheels/tyres leaned in

towards each other - not a pretty sight. And talking of pretty sights (not), the dashboard in the van had been made out of plywood sheet, I guess, and covered in brown velour with brocade trim! Overall it had already acquired that patina of neglect that could easily have marked the start of a terminal decline.

A couple of changes of owner later, its whereabouts

The only photograph we've ever seen of the van showing its gullwing doors. Our estimation is that it would be 12' 2" wide with both doors open!

and availability became known to Nigel Stanley, a hot rod and custom car enthusiast who had none of my reservations. By this time the van had become an even more difficult proposition to rebuild - stock or otherwise - and its destiny could easily have been the nearest scrapyard. Luckily that's not the way Nigel saw it. He imagined it with wider arches, neat body beautifully painted and detailed but nothing dramatic like a top chop, a sensible engine/gearbox combination (when purchased it had had the gas-guzzling V8 removed) - a very 'retro' custom was planned. Nigel's choice of motor was a Granada V6 coupled to an auto gearbox; an unusual choice - two cylinders too many if you're a classic purist, two too few if you're a dedicated hot-rodder! The auto box was essential really; there just was not enough room in the footwell for three pedals, partly because the engine/gearbox combination was mounted on the chassis centreline (unlike the offset of the original) and also because of the added width of the V6. A Granada was also to provide the front axle/suspension etc. as well as the two front seats.

Burnham Autos, of Northfleet, were entrusted with the task of turning Nigel's master plan into a masterpiece - an undertaking that they coped with admirably. All sorts of changes were incorporated along the way. There are so many beautiful touches; some

As acquired by Nigel. Running boards, Beetle rear lights and front doors now hung 'suicide' style -hinged down their trailing edges. You'd need some vision!

discreet, like the mechanisms for locking the sliding doors (always a weakness of the standard van) which are hidden within the double skin of the standard steel doors; others more overt, like the gas shocks which can raise or lower the body on its suspension at the touch of a button. Nigel's original idea for the paint scheme was to use dark blue and cream (Morris-Commercial's house style) but unusually have the darker colour on the top half. This was to change when he drove past a VW van in two-tone cream. The paint finish is a triumph of the spraygun, and on opening the rear doors, the fully carpeted and fabric-covered interior matches the exterior in its use of the same two tones, and in the way that it follows the body's waistline. So much care has been lavished upon every last detail. The rebuild went according to plan but not to schedule, but the result has made all of the delays worthwhile.

Being taken for a spin round the block (well two or three blocks, actually, by the time I'd taken it all in) was such a treat! This is like no other J-type. For instance, it has in-car entertainment - and you can enjoy it, thanks to the sound deadening/carpeting. The only way you can listen to music in an ordinary J, is if you happen to be sat at traffic lights with your door open, alongside someone with a very loud system.

No doubt there are purists out there who might say that this shouldn't happen to a J-type. I would say that here is another J returned to the streets, where it should be - a van previously compromised by some far more radical customising, saved by Nigel's timely intervention. And, best of all, it's used nearly every day.

A wonderful advert for Nigel's business.

Hovis Loaf
Meets
American Graffiti!

344 CNM - Work in Progress

Left and above: Before and after shots showing the nearside body repair. Complete replacement lower panels were wheeled for both sides. The hot rod in the background illustrates the more radical stuff that usually goes through Burnham's workshops. The cardboard construction on the floor is a template for a custom-made fuel tank.

Above: Offside lower body repair. Replacement inner wings were fabricated for both sides.

Right: The engine cover under construction, a work of art in itself.

Right: Finally some paint goes on, and even in primer it is starting to look special.

Left: Repairs to the front end included a new lower valance panel to the original pattern and metal let into the front wings where holes had been cut, by a previous owner, for indicators.

Above: The custom fascia, fully painted up and being fitted out. Instruments from an early Mini were used to keep the retro feel.

Right: The signwriter has done his job beautifully, and the point has been reached where panels and glass can now be refitted.

In 1948....

The dawn of a New Era!

The Earls Court Motor Show was the first since 1938. Over half a million people attended, compared with fewer than a quarter of a million for the previous one. Eleven major new models were announced. The Morris Minor was described by Autocar as 'a real triumph of British design'. It had a purchase price of £280.0.0 + Purchase tax, which brought it to a total of £358.10.7d. Also introduced were the Hillman Minx, the Austin A70, and the Morris Oxford saloon - the Minor's 'big brother', whilst Jaguar introduced one of the surprises of the show, the XK120 Roadster, to the public. Originally intended as a batch of 200 aluminium-bodied cars, it was soon realised that this would not meet the demand, and the decision was taken to tool up for a pressed steel body. Wolseley, another great British marque, introduced their Four-Fifty and Six-Eighty models.

In 'The Field' in November 1948, Sir Malcolm Cambell wrote, with some frustration, *"Here were displayed all that is latest and best in the way of British and foreign motor-car production, teeming with attraction for the car-starved would-be purchasers of cars to replace the outworn and out-moded models that have served us so well since 1939. But everywhere one was confronted with the forbidding signs: "For Export Only," or "For Exhibition Only." Here and there enquiry as to the possibility of acquiring a new car would be met with the cautious pronouncement: "Well, perhaps some time next year."*

The Rover Company introduced the Land Rover at the 1948 Amsterdam Motor Show. It was originally intended as a stop gap, a vehicle that they could produce during the post-war period of steel rationing and which would keep the company going until it was allowed to return to car production. Price of the vehicle only, without additional equipment was £450.

with a much smaller allowance than previously, limiting an individual's travel to 90 miles a week. Rationing ended in 1957.

The 18th of September saw the return of motor racing to post-war Britain, long after the sport had restarted in other European countries. The 2.4 mile circuit at Goodwood hosted this first meeting, the opening race of which was won by Paul Pycroft in an SS100 Jaguar. Stirling Moss, at the time relatively unknown except in hill-climb circles, won the 500cc event. The main race, for the newly formed 'formula 1' cars, was won by Reg Parnell in a Maserati 4CLT/48

Norton Motors had been in existence for 50 years, having started producing motorcycle parts in Bradford Street, in Birmingham, in 1898. In the Isle of Man TT the Norton trio of Bell, Doran and Weddell came in first, second and third in the senior (500cc) race.

Ferrari, the Italian sports car manufacturer, celebrated its 1st birthday!

A gallon of petrol cost 2s 1d. For the first five months of 1948 petrol was unavailable to the private motorist, following the withdrawal of petrol rations late in 1947. Coupons became available again from June 1st, but

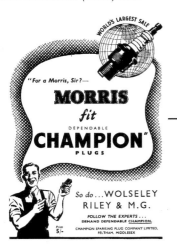

The front cover of the programme for the first postwar motor race in England, at Goodwood.

On January 1st, the four main railway companies - GWR, LMS, LNER and Southern - were nationalised and became British Railways. It was still possible to travel 3rd Class on the Railways, which was not abolished until 1956!

The British gas and electricity industries were nationalised, following on from the nationalisation of the coal mines in 1947 and the Bank of England in 1946.

Bread rationing ended in Britain. A loaf of bread cost 41/2d

Soap was still rationed. 1950 saw the end.

The first Oxfam shop opened in Broad Street, Oxford.

On July 4th the National Health Service came into being, following an agreement to co-operate being reached with the British Medical Association

A bottle of White Horse scotch "I think I'd like a White Horse better than anything" was 31/- (£1.55) in January, but by June had risen to 33/4 - prices fixed by the Scotch Whisky Association.

Proposals for a £2,000,000,000 annual lottery, as an aid to national recovery, were submitted to the Prime Minister and the Chancellor of the Exchequer. Nearly 50 years later the idea was taken seriously......

The continuance of compulsary military service was secured by the National Service Bill. It only ended in 1960.

Britain's first supermarket was opened by the London Co-operative Society in Manor Park.

The Crown Jewels were returned to the Tower of London following their removal, for reasons of security, shortly after the outbreak of the Second World War, in 1939.

Clothes rationing was still in existence. It ended in 1949.

The National Insurance Act introduced a compulsory system of employee and employer contributions, which previously had been voluntary.

The Poor Law was replaced by National Assistance.

Mahatma Gandhi was assassinated by a Hindu extremist in New Delhi, whilst fasting to promote peace between Hindus and Moslems.

What the well-dressed J-type owner should be wearing?

The International Planned Parenthood Federation was launched by Margaret Stanger, a crusading enthusiast of family planning. As long ago as 1916, she had opened the first birth control centre - in Brooklyn - although it was soon closed down by the New York police as a 'public nuisance'

The Naturist Foundation was formed (sorry, we can't find a relevant picture!).

Burma became an independent Republic.

Harry S Truman was elected US President.

The new state of Israel was proclaimed by the Jews.

Following a coup, Communist leaders formed a new Government in Czechoslovak ia.

The "Berlin Airlift" was required, after Allied zones had supplies cut off by the USSR preventing road and rail traffic.

Polos, the mint with the hole, were introduced to the marketplace on the 15th April 1948. The polo was originally described as 'the peppermint ring made wholly by Rowntrees'. Cute slogan, huh! They cost 1d a pack, and were only available initially in London and the south-east. The year also saw the introduction of Walkers crisps.

Postal charges were tuppence ha'penny (roughly 1P in today's decimal coinage) for a letter not exceeding 2 ounces, plus one halfpenny for every additional 2 ounces or part thereof. Postcards - Inland and Abroad, including HM Forces and ships of war, were two pence single or four pence for Reply Paid (amounting to a two pence stamp on each part). The Post Office published 2

new sets of stamps (a far cry from the present when new sets come out with an alarming frequency). The first set was a pair of stamps commemorating the Royal Silver Wedding. These 2½d and £1 stamps came out on 26th April. On 29th July four stamps were introduced to celebrate, and to coincide with, the opening of the Olympic Games. *The 1948 Olympic Games, the first*

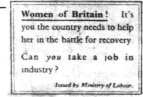

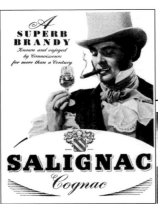

Although the advertisement dates from 1948, and perhaps much earlier, its use on the roof of this J–type came about in 1951. The highly skilled artist at The Paragon Motor Co. Ltd. carried out the job with the roof of the van having been removed and placed on an easel!

since 1936, were held in London. King George opened them at Wembley Stadium on July 29th. The banners of 59 nations were in the march past, both Germany and Japan being absent. The Czech Emil Zatopek became the instant hero, winning the 10,000m by a three quarter lap margin - and winning the silver medal in the 5,000m. Heroine of the women's events was the Dutch athlete Fanny Blankers-Koen, who took gold in the 100m, 200m, 80m hurdles and in the relay. She was 30 years old at the time and had competed in the Berlin Olympics 12 years before. The leader of the Czech women's contingent claimed political refugee status, and refused to return to Czechoslovakia.

'My Love' at 100 to 9 won the Derby, ridden by W Johnstone. It was owned by H H Aga Khan and M L Volterra 'Sheila's Cottage' won the Grand National, ridden by A P Thompson.

There were 43 runners, equalling the previous third-largest field in 1931.

Lester Piggott won his first race, at the age of 14!

The 94th Boat Race between Oxford and Cambridge saw Cambridge win by 5 lengths, in a time of 17 minutes and 50 seconds. This record time stood until 1974, when the Oxford crew shaved 15 seconds off the 1948 time.

Joe Louis retired from boxing, after fighting 25 title bouts since 1937. Londoner Freddie Mills narrowly beat Gus Lesnevich to win the world light-heavyweight title at the White City stadium.

The 1st Division Champions (this was long before a Premier League was thought of) were Arsenal, with Manchester United second. Coincidentally, in 1998 - the 50th anniversary of the introduction of the J-type - the very same happened at the end of the Premier League season! Such symmetry!

Stanley Matthews (1915-2000) was Footballer of the Year. Stanley's death robbed 'the beautiful game' of a true ambassador and gentleman.

The FA Cup was won by Manchester United, who beat Blackpool 4-2.

TV had just the one channel, and was only available within a radius of approximately 45 miles of London. The BBC Television Service was broadcast each evening from 8.30 onwards. The ten o'clock news was relayed in sound only as an economy measure. There were fewer than 55,000 television licences issued, roughly 1 in 1000 of the population of the British Isles.

The word 'Scrabble' appeared in the Collins English Dictionary for the first time. 'Kan-U-Go' was a similar, but ultimately less successful, word game.

Commercial TV did not begin until 1955, with Gibbs SR toothpaste being the product first advertised.

The BBC's radio services consisted of the Home Service - broadcast on medium wave and organised on a local basis, the Light Programme and the Third Programme, plus the European and Overseas Services.

There were approximately 5 million telephones in use in the British Isles!

The Long-playing record, which needed totally new equipment to play, was announced by Columbia Records at a press conference in New York in June 1948. The CBS research team, under Dr. Peter Goldmark, came up with a record made of unbreakable plastic rather than the previous shellac, which revolved at 33rpm instead of 78rpm. The LP was not introduced into Britain until 1950 when it was launched by Decca. Stereo recording was being developed, but was not a marketable reality until the late '50s.

The transistor was first demonstrated by William Shockley, John Bardeen and Walter Brattain at the Bell Telephone Laboratories in the U.S. It could do virtually all the jobs of conventional radio valves, but was more reliable, more rugged, smaller and required only a fraction as much power. The valve was on its way out.

No one knew of 'The Mousetrap'! Agatha Christie's play did not open until 1952. Children had no idea of the delights that Noddy would bring to them. Enid Blyton's first book in the series, 'Noddy goes to Toyland' was to appear in 1949.

1948 GEC portable

Taken in 1954, this photo is of a J-type being loaded into a Silver City Airways Freighter. It would appear to be quite a tight fit! Peter Moor, Morris-Commercial Dealer and ex-apprentice, used this J-type for a holiday in France, taking along 11 other people and their luggage! The passengers were three Honiton families, six adults and six children, accomodated by the addition of two bucket seats from a Morris Eight and the use of suitably padded cabin trunks. 1,006 miles were covered with an average petrol consumption of 28 mpg. Quite an undertaking in a sidevalve 'J'!

Silver City Airways introduced their car ferry across the English Channel on July 14th, using Bristol Type 170 Freighters - extremely tough and versatile airplanes. Flights operated four times a day between Lympne in Kent and Le Touquet, with flying time of under 20 minutes between terminals. The very first car to use the service was an Armstrong-Siddeley, registered HXN 88, which was flown over the Channel in Freighter G-AGVC. Over the next 10 years, Silver City Freighters travelled 125,000 miles to and fro across the Channel carrying 215,000 cars and 759,000 passengers.

Work was well underway on two prototypes, but it would be another year before the De Havilland Comet, the first jet airliner to be awarded a Certificate of Airworthiness, made its first test flight in July '49. Making first flights in '48 were the Handley Page Hermes IV and the Vickers Viscount, whilst Britain's first multi-jet tailless aircraft, the Armstrong Whitworth AW 52 was undergoing flight trials.

And, of course, most importantly, Morris-Commercial (who had only been in existance for 24 years - but who could justify even then the claim to 'Britain's largest factory specialising exclusively in commercial vehicles') introduced the J-type 10 cwt Express Delivery van, the jewel in the Morris-Commercial crown, to an eager audience at the 14th International Commercial Motor Transport Exhibition, at Earls Court. Production of the J-type would not start for some months and most of the early vehicles went for export.

It was
one remarkable year!

The AW52 undergoing flight trials. State-of-the-art aviation then, which still looks space-age today!

DINKY

Dinky 260
'Royal Mail'
- red body, wings and wheels.
(at least two versions,
sometimes with black roof).

Dinky 299
The **'Royal Mail'** van was also available in a
gift set with a **'Post Office Telephones'** Z
van, along with Telephone box, messenger
and postman.

Dinky 465
'Capstan'
- light blue upper body and
front wings, dark blue lower
body, grille panel and rear
wings plus mid blue wheels.

In the
1950s and '60s,
when J-types
were still a
common sight
on the roads –
delivering the
mail, the milk,
bread and all
sorts of other
goods – they
were certainly
not so common
a sight in
toyshops.
There was very
little to choose
from by way of
models.

J, JB & 101 REGISTER ARCHIVES

Triang Minic
Available as **'Royal Mail'** (red),
'Post Office Telephones' (green)
"Minic Transport (red)"and
in a light blue/grey with no
signwriting.

Triang
'Macleans' Toothpaste
- white and light blue based
on a real vehicle which was
built on a
J-type chassis by
Commercial Motors (Harrow).

A remarkable vehicle and an

unusual subject for a model!

TRIANG/MINIC

In the early '90s
Corgi were to
change all
that......

No attempt has been made to illustrate the
following Corgi models in
their chronological order.
I thought it preferable to show the models
with known correct liveries first,
then the rest in a
'descending order of believability'.

Collecting
J-types
in Miniature!

CORGI

The first two Corgi releases were the Royal Mail and Post Office Telephones vans – genuine liveries but with some inaccuracies. It is certainly disappointing that no attempt was made to make realistic representations of the wheels, even though those on other models in the range are perfectly accurate.

All of the models on this page carry known correct liveries.

Other **'Royal Mail'** variants include:

POV 21
96882
and 06203

D983/2
'Royal Mail' "ER"
- red body with black roof and wings, no silver paint to simulate chrome on the grille detail.

D983/1
'Post Office Telephones'
(based on the Bowkett's RGK 633) - mid bronze green body with black wings and incorrect grey roof.

99140
'Post Office Telephones'
(RGK 633) - mid bronze green body (and roof) with black wings and wheels + printed posterboards.

97735
'Cumberland Pencil Co'
(part of Cumbrian set, with Bedford box van) - red body, cream detail with black wings and wheels. (NRM 284)

97200
'BRS Parcels Services'
(part of set exclusive to Kay's catalogue) - green body with black roof and wings.

96891
'Morris Service'
(Ed Morgan's OAD 41) - cream upper body, dark blue lower body and wings (which should be black!)

06204
'RAC Sign Service'
- mid blue body with black wings Silver painted hubcaps on black wheels.
(LDG 584 - in RAC collection)

D983/5
'Walls Ice Cream'
- cream upper body, light blue lower body with black wings.
(re-run with code 98101)

96888
'Southdown'
- green body and wheels, with black wings + 2 unpainted figures.

CORGI

D46/1
'British Railways'
(part of set with Bedford box van)
- maroon body and wings with black
roof.

D983/4
'Metropolitan Police'
- dark blue body with black wings
and roof.

96880
'Pickfords'
- dark blue body and
wings with white signwriting.
(re-run with code no. 99802)

Who would have guessed that Corgi, when they brought out their model of the J-type in the early '90s, would end up doing so many different versions of it. This chapter illustrates this orgy of marketing excess – 32 different liveries ranging from the accurate to the just plain absurd!

31002
'National Benzole'
(part of set with Foden FG Tanker)
- yellow body with black wings.
Silver painted hubcaps on black
wheels.

97695
'BMC Competitions Department'
(part of Abingdon set, with 2 MGAs)
- British racing green with black
wings and roof.

96895
**'Birmingham Corporation
Transport'**
- cream upper/dark blue lower body
with sand colour roof and black
wings.

A number of the 96895 **'Birmingham Corporation Transport'** went out with the words 'Genetal Manager' rather than 'General Manager' as part of the small lettering on the lower body sides. These are much sought after by collectors. The vehicles in the Birmingham Corporation Transport fleet were all-over dark blue, unlike the Corgi model which transposes a bus livery onto the van.

D54/1
'Electricity'
(part of gift set with CA, Minor and
Ford 5cwt, exclusive to GUS
catalogue) - grey body with black
roof and wings.

97746
'Corgi'
(part of Toymaster set, paired with
Bedford CA) - mid blue body and
wings, red lettering and logo.

96886
'Family Assurance'
- cream upper body, brick red lower
body and wings.

CORGI

Better wheels and front grille insert, along with small modifications to the chassis to prevent the model's natural desire to sag, (why, oh why, did Corgi decide to fit this unsuccessful form of suspension?) could rejuvenate this model.

97765
'W Forbes'
(part of Strathblair set, with Bedford OB coach) - blue body with black wings.

08007
'Cadbury's Cocoa'
(part of set, with Bedford CA) - dark red body and wheels, with black wings.

06205
'Royal Worcester'
- green body, cream roof and wings with black wheels with silver painted centres.

97714
'Royal Air Force'
(part of RAF set)
- white upper body and wings, light blue/grey lower body with black wheels.

06201
'Cydrax'
- apple green body and wheels, black wings.

96892
'Bovril'
- warm red body with black wings.

06202
'Beefy Oxo'
- blue body and wheels with black wings.

D983/3
'Corgi Collectors Club 1991'
(only available to club members)
- yellow upper body, blue lower body and roof with black wings.

CC06202
Nottingham City Ambulance Service cream with green wheels and waistline stripe
Carries registration no. SAU 936

96887
'The Topper'
- Old English white body with red wings and body-side feature.

98758
'The Wizard'
- red upper, yellow lower body with black wings.

5D983/7
'Minnie the Minx'
- cream with black wings.
(part of gift set D47/1 with AEC double decker bus)

98759/B
'The Dandy/Korky the Cat'
(part of set 98759, with Bedford CA)
- cream upper, mid blue lower body with black wings.

98660/B
'The Beano/Beryl the Peril'
(part of set 98960, with Morris Minor LCV) - light blue upper body and wings,
pale cream lower body.

98970/B
'The X-Men'
(part of set 98970, with Bedford CA)
- green upper body with pale green lower body and wings.

98972/B
'Spiderman'
(part of set 98972)
- lilac body with dark blue wings.

Colourful they might be, but the 'Comic Book Heroes' vans could certainly not be described as realistic!

With so many restored vans, so much variety within the basic vehicles and so many known liveries, let's hope that Corgi return to making some new ones!

The 'X-Men' gift set appears in the January - June 1992 Corgi Classic brochure with both vehicles in entirely different colour schemes from how they appeared in production, the 'J'type sporting an orange body and blue wheelarches. None are believed to have been sold in this alternative scheme.

From time to time smaller companies have attempted to fill the gaps by introducing models made from white metal or plastic, in various scales.

A Smith Models
1:48 'Dinky copy' four known versions.

Maru San (Japanese)
1:48 'Dinky copy' one known version.

Dinkum Models (Australian)
1:48 'Dinky copy' with modifications, one known version.

Ertl/Thomas and Friends
'Sodor Mail Van' Gauge unknown, plastic van   not specifically a J-type but with lots of J-type proportion and detailing.

Roadscale Models
00 gauge, white metal kit with poor detailing particularly around front grille.

The Classic Model Company
00 gauge, plastic kit with excellent detailing.

Tober Models
1:43, one version known, Royal Mail.

Pathfinder Models
1:43, five or six versions - all civilian liveries.

Crossway Models
1:43, GPO Planners van, modelled on Ray Kings' 949 BYY. This carries full interior detail and is a much modified *Pathfinders Models* van.

Other Known Models

Fancy something a bit different in your collection? This unfinished model of Ray Binelli's van (still in daily use in London) is made up from two Corgi models. An ice cream van could be made in the same way.

R DOIG

A Code 3 van was produced to promote the Wolseley 6/80 and Morris Oxford Club, many years ago.
It was in light and dark blue.

Code 3 vans were sold by Angel Miniatures who applied transfers to models supplied by Corgi. Known to us are:
'Players Navy Cut'   'Fyffes'
'Dunlop'   'Red Cross Ambulance'   'Valor'
'Ovaltine'
'Military Ambulance'
'Schweppes'
'England's Glory'   'Royal Mail' 'Whitbreads'

This van by Roslyn Models of Hull, carries the registration number NRH 144, that of a real vehicle purchased new from Paragon Motors and which clocked up nearly 100,000 miles.

Thanks to
Bill McMahon,
Roger de Boer,
Iain McKenzie, Rod Harper,
Mike Bell (who trusted me with hundreds of pounds worth of models)
and Paul Kennelly at
Time Machine, Coventry
for their help in the compilation of this chapter

This Code 3 model was made for the members of the Coventry Diecast Model Club, and featured this neat illustration on its unique box.

CODE 3
CORGI

Many Code 3 models have been introduced since Corgi brought out their J-type model in 1992. It would be impossible for us to list them all, so we have only aimed at illustrating a selection of those available.

ILLUSTRATION BY 'HOAGY' BURTON

OTHER

Where do you stop when collecting J-types in miniature? All of these qualify, from the hand-built pedal car to the teapot!

This pedal-powered J-type was made by the author in roughly one-quarter scale. Whilst the original was made in wood, a number of GRP copies have been made, one of which has been turned into a battery-powered miniature masterpiece by trainees at LDV!

We have no idea whether any of these items are still in production, but searching them out can be fun.

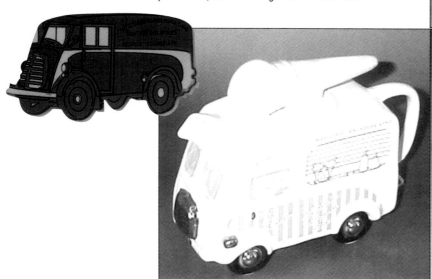

OTHER

Why stop at models? There are postcards, badges, keyfobs, jigsaws, old photographs, manuals, sales literature and all sorts of ephemera out there.

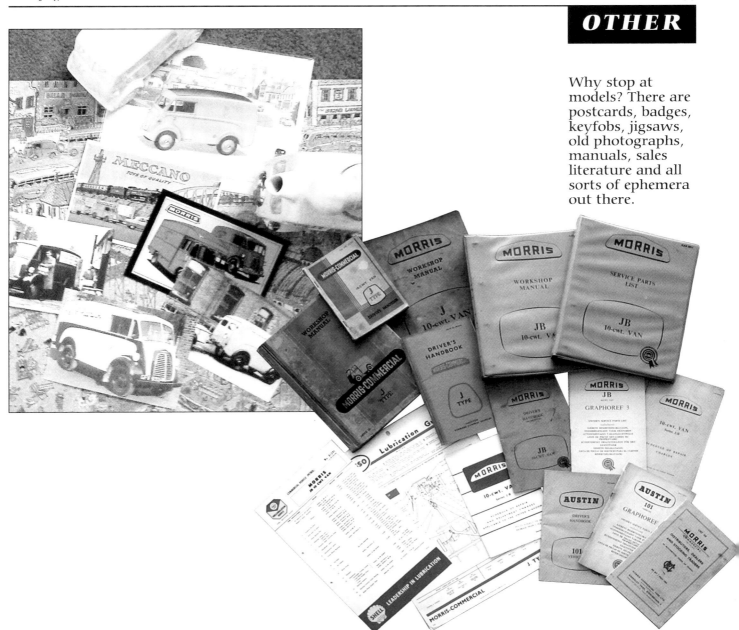

Ouch – It shouldn't happen to a J-type!

CJE 723 was registered to Wisbech Rural District Council on October the 17th, 1952.

The chassis number is not recorded, only that the van was blue. It is known that the registration number was cancelled on the 28th of January, 1964, although this may not be any clue as to when the accident occurred. Despite the severity of the situation, the body does not look to be badly damaged and the van could well have been repaired and returned to service. Nothing is known about the accident, or whose ownership the vehicle was in when it occurred.

What nostalgia the pictures evoke. This was an age when grown-ups wore hats and front gardens were edged with neatly clipped privet. Bicycles had big spoked wheels with thin tyres, scooters had proper-sized wheels, and kids wore cowboy suits. One lad's lucky enough to have a toy revolver and holster - no 'pyaww- pyaaw' and pointing of fingers for him - little wonder the girl is looking in awe.   Police cars were black and chimneys didn't bristle with aerials, much less satellite dishes.

Might the outcome have been different had the Council paid extra to have the optional bumpers?

Both of these photographs are published with the kind permission of the Lilian Ream Collection, Cambridgeshire.

Bedford CA

From 1952 the J-type had direct competition from the Bedford CA, similar in size and layout - including the offset engine. Bedford engineers were happy to place more trust in the prop shaft's u-joints than did their Morris-Commercial counterparts, since they kept the differential central in the rear axle. This simplified the manufacture of left-hand drive versions but did put the prop shaft at an unusual angle. The CA was designated as a 10-12 cwt van. Although six inches wider and three inches longer than a J-type, the CA could only manage 135 cu ft of load-carrying space. Perhaps due to its slightly more modern styling, having come later to the marketplace, the CA soldiered on until 1969 - by which time it was looking a bit long in the tooth but had passed the 370,000 mark in worldwide sales!

Length overall: 3905mm
Width: 1775mm
height: 1905mm
Wheelbase: 2286mm
Load Bed height: 635mm

Ford E83W

The E83W was fitted with a sidevalve 4-cylinder engine coupled to a 3-speed gearbox. Its engine was offset slightly from the chassis centreline, allowing a semi-forward control driving position. Between 1938 and 1957, Ford produced more than 188,00 of these models.

Length overall: 4000mm
Width: 1625mm
height: 1867mm
Wheelbase: 2286mm

An entirely new van, fully forward control, was introduced in 1957, designated the 400E. This had a 52bhp engine, and was well received by delivery drivers.

Length overall: 4077mm
Width: 1791mm
height: 1994mm
Wheelbase: 2133mm

Volkswagen Type 2   # DKW Schnellaster

Production of the box van, Kombi and Bus started in 1950, followed by the Samba Bus in 1951 and the Open Truck in 1952. Many other variants followed, including a High Roof Box Van, Double Cab Pickup Truck and a Wide Body Wooden Pickup.

By 1967, when the split-screen model was replaced with the single curved-screen 'bay window' van, 1,853,439 of this type had been manufactured. That is more than 1.8 million MORE than the total 11 year production run of the J-type, and equates to 38 VWs for every one J made!

Length overall: 4190mm
Width: 1725mm(van) 1710mm(pickup)
height: 1900mm (van)
Wheelbase: 2400mm
Load Bed height: 480mm
Load Limit: 800kg

In production from 1949 through to 1962, 58,792 of the Schnellaster (Quick-Loader) were manufactured. Both vans and trucks were produced, with a load carrying limit of 3/4 ton. Performance must have been poor, since the vehicle was equipped with a 2-cylinder, 20 horsepower, 690 cc engine!

These vehicles had single-piece flat glass windscreens incorporated into surprisingly curvy front panels.

Length overall: 3870mm
Width: 1550mm(van) 1600mm(pickup)
height: 1580mm
Wheelbase: 2500mm
Load Bed height: 300mm
Load Limit: 750kg

All dimensions have been rounded up/down to the nearest whole number.
Comparative figures for the J-type are on page 2.

There's no better sight than a J-type in its natural environment - on the road - seeing five in convoy is positively thrilling!

The Current Scene

Worldwide, around 500 J-types are known to have survived, roughly 1% of the production total. Many of these are in regular use, particularly during the rally season. A very few are still in daily use with their owners, earning their keep by transporting goods and promoting the business! The Cumberland Pencil Company still have a J-type which they have owned from new. The van is occasionally used for local deliveries, and can be seen outside their Museum at Keswick, in Cumbria, as a static display.

J-types very occasionally appear for sale in the 'J-type Review', the newsletter of the J, JB and 101 Register and in the classic car press. These are usually snapped up very quickly. More vehicles in very poor condition are now being restored as the supply of better prospects diminish. One J-type owner, enthusiast and member of the Register, Iain McKenzie, is now making many repair panels for these vans. Thanks to his sterling efforts, many a desicion to restore rather than break for spares may now be taken.

Keeping a 'J' On The Road

As it is over 40 years since production of the J-type ceased, it is generally necessary to search at autojumbles and/or use the services of specialist obsolete parts suppliers for many components. Some parts are common to other BMC vehicles, whilst others may be similar enough to allow use with minor modifications. It is a surprise to occasionally find the odd part still available off-the-shelf, such as wheel bearings and water pumps.

Owners Modifications

J-types quite often had their side-valve engines and 3-speed gearboxes replaced by B series engines and 4-speed 'boxes during their working life, because of the considerable improvements that this brought

about. Sometimes very early vans are found to have the later type axle fitted. To make the J-type and the J/B more suitable for longer journeys, owners have been known to swap the crown wheel and pinion in the differential for a more suitable ratio.

In a similar quest for improvement, and bearing in mind the changing traffic conditions and that these vans are rarely used for the sort of local delivery work for which they were designed, many owners have made further changes to their vans.

We know of:

A 'J' pick-up with 1500 B series diesel and an auto box.

An Austin 101 with an 1800cc Freight Rover engine and 5-speed box.

A 101 with an 1800cc B series engine (from a Morris Marina) coupled to a Ford Sierra 5-speed box, using a conversion kit manufactured by a specialist company.

A 'J' with 1800cc MG engine (again a B series) complete with its 4-speed box and overdrive.

Each of these conversions keeps the character of the J-type intact, whilst allowing 21st-Century motoring enjoyment from vans half a century old!

MGB-powered 'J' van, owned by Iain Booth in New Zealand. Iain originally fitted a mid-mounted V8, but subsequently decided on something nearer to the original. Fitting-out will soon see it back on the road!

My thanks to:
Richard Maclaurin
Don Foster
POVC (esp. Mark Skillen and Chris Hogan)
BT Archives
The Lilian Ream Collection
BMIHT (Gaydon)
Bob Sandford
Sean Carrara & Shesha Courtney
Gary Sutton
Nigel Stanley
Chris Salaman
Mike Sutcliffe
Mike Bell
Roger de Boer
Geoff Fishwick
Graham Swales
Richard Hunt
Peter Devoti at Granelli's
Mike Greenwood
Ken Bennett
Ken Cooke
Graham Southard
Peter Seaword
Roland Turner
Graham Wilton
Peter Bateman
Jon Thompson/Split Screen Van Club
Whitby Specialist Vehicles
Jess Hogan
and all who have helped with information
and encouragement for this project.

Please forgive any possible omissions.
Every effort has been made to include all
organisations and individuals involved in
the book.

This book is dedicated to my wife Bezzie,
and my children Laura, Joel and Abigail,
who have shown patience beyond
measure, and support for which I will
always be thankful.

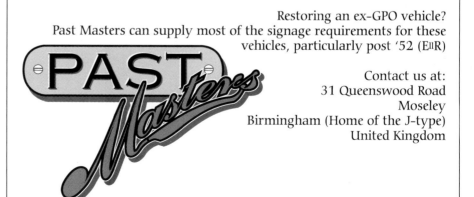